RUIZ 11/28/06

Put Beginning Readers on the Right Track with
ALL ABOARD READING™

The All Aboard Reading series is especially designed for beginning readers. Written by noted authors and illustrated in full color, these are books that children really want to read—books to excite their imagination, expand their interests, make them laugh, and support their feelings. With fiction and nonfiction stories that are high interest and curriculum-related, All Aboard Reading books offer something for every young reader. And with four different reading levels, the All Aboard Reading series lets you choose which books are most appropriate for your children and their growing abilities.

Picture Readers
Picture Readers have super-simple texts, with many nouns appearing as rebus pictures. At the end of each book are 24 flash cards—on one side is a rebus picture; on the other side is the written-out word.

Station Stop 1
Station Stop 1 books are best for children who have just begun to read. Simple words and big type make these early reading experiences more comfortable. Picture clues help children to figure out the words on the page. Lots of repetition throughout the text helps children to predict the next word or phrase—an essential step in developing word recognition.

Station Stop 2
Station Stop 2 books are written specifically for children who are reading with help. Short sentences make it easier for early readers to understand what they are reading. Simple plots and simple dialogue help children with reading comprehension.

Station Stop 3
Station Stop 3 books are perfect for children who are reading alone. With longer text and harder words, these books appeal to children who have mastered basic reading skills. More complex stories captivate children who are ready for more challenging books.

In addition to All Aboard Reading books, look for All Aboard Math Readers™ (fiction stories that teach math concepts children are learning in school); All Aboard Science Readers™ (nonfiction books that explore the most fascinating science topics in age-appropriate language); All Aboard Poetry Readers™ (funny, rhyming poems for readers of all levels); and All Aboard Mystery Readers™ (puzzling tales where children piece together evidence with the characters).

All Aboard for happy reading!

GROSSET & DUNLAP
Published by the Penguin Group
Penguin Group (USA) Inc., 375 Hudson Street, New York, New York 10014, U.S.A.
Penguin Group (Canada), 90 Eglinton Avenue East, Suite 700,
Toronto, Ontario, Canada M4P 2Y3
(a division of Pearson Penguin Canada Inc.)
Penguin Books Ltd, 80 Strand, London WC2R 0RL, England
Penguin Ireland, 25 St Stephen's Green, Dublin 2, Ireland
(a division of Penguin Books Ltd)
Penguin Group (Australia), 250 Camberwell Road, Camberwell, Victoria 3124, Australia
(a division of Pearson Australia Group Pty Ltd)
Penguin Books India Pvt Ltd, 11 Community Centre, Panchsheel Park,
New Delhi—110 017, India
Penguin Group (NZ), Cnr Airborne and Rosedale Roads, Albany, Auckland 1310, New Zealand
(a division of Pearson New Zealand Ltd)
Penguin Books (South Africa) (Pty) Ltd, 24 Sturdee Avenue, Rosebank,
Johannesburg 2196, South Africa

Penguin Books Ltd, Registered Offices:
80 Strand, London WC2R 0RL, England

Library of Congress Cataloging-in-Publication Data

Holabird, Katharine.
Angelina has the hiccups! / by Katharine Holabird ; based on the illustrations by Helen Craig.
    p. cm. — (All aboard reading. Station stop 1)
Summary: Angelina is devastated when, after practicing very hard for her role as head flower princess in the big recital, she develops hiccups on the night of the performance.
ISBN 0-448-44389-9 (pbk.)
    [1. Mice—Fiction. 2. Ballet dancing—Fiction. 3. Hiccups—Fiction.] I. Craig, Helen. II. Title. III. Series.
PZ7.H689All 2006
[E]—dc22
                2006002436

10 9 8 7 6 5 4 3 2 1

Angelina Has the Hiccups!

By Katharine Holabird
Based on the illustrations by Helen Craig

Grosset & Dunlap

Angelina loves to dance.

Angelina dances

on the way to school . . .

in the playground . . .

even at bedtime!

Angelina has a very best friend.

Her name is Alice.

Alice loves to dance, too.

Angelina and Alice go

to ballet school every week.

Their teacher is Miss Lilly.

Angelina and Alice

love Miss Lilly.

Today Miss Lilly has a surprise.

"We will give a performance,"

she tells the class.

"The dance is called
*The Flower Princesses
and the Dragon.*"
"Yippee!" everyone shouts.

13

All the ballet students are
in the show.

Cousin Henry is the dragon.

"ROAR!" Henry roars proudly.

"I am a very scary dragon."

Angelina and the other mouselings
are flower princesses.

Angelina is Rose.

She has a wand with a rose.

Alice is Violet.

Her wand has a violet on top.

Miss Lilly shows her students
the steps in the dance.
The flower princesses twirl and
leap across the room.

Henry the dragon
takes big dragon steps.
Thud! Thud! Thud!
"Practice makes perfect,"
Miss Lilly says.

Every morning, Angelina
gets up early.

"Watch me twirl and leap,"
she says.

"Not in the kitchen!"

Mrs. Mouseling reminds her.

Every day after school,

Angelina and Alice practice.

They know all

the steps by heart.

Today the mouselings try
on their costumes.
"What if I forget the steps?"
says Alice.
Angelina says,
"Do not worry.
Just follow me."

Now Alice feels much better.

Henry has his costume, too.

But he will not let anyone see it.

"I want it to be a surprise,"

he says.

On the day of the show,

Angelina is very excited.

Soon Alice arrives.

"Hi," says Alice.

"Hi!" says Angelina.

Then out comes a big—

HICCUP!

Hiccup! Hiccup! Hiccup!

Oh, no!

Angelina has the hiccups.

"Hold your breath," says Alice.

Angelina holds her breath.

"HICCUP!" she hiccups.

"Try a spoonful of sugar,"
says Mrs. Mouseling.
Angelina eats a spoonful
of sugar.
"HICCUP!" Angelina hiccups.
Then Angelina hiccups
all the way to the theater.

"Blow in a paper bag,"

says Miss Lilly.

Angelina blows in a paper bag.

"HICCUP!" she hiccups.

Angelina puts on her costume.

HICCUP!

Angelina puts on her
ballet slippers.

HICCUP!

Angelina gets her rose wand.

HICCUP!

The music is starting.

"HICCUP!" Angelina hiccups.

Angelina is ready to cry.

How can she be a

hiccuping ballerina?

"ROAR!"

A scary dragon jumps out

at Angelina.

Angelina jumps, too.

But it is only Henry—

Henry the dragon!

"I told Henry to try scaring

away your hiccups,"

says Alice.

"Did it work?"

Angelina smiles.

No more hiccups!

On stage, Angelina and Alice
twirl and leap.

The flower princesses turn
the scary dragon into
a friendly dragon.

After the dance,

Angelina hugs Henry.

"Thank you," she says.

"ROAR!" Henry roars proudly.